This book belongs to:

. . . .

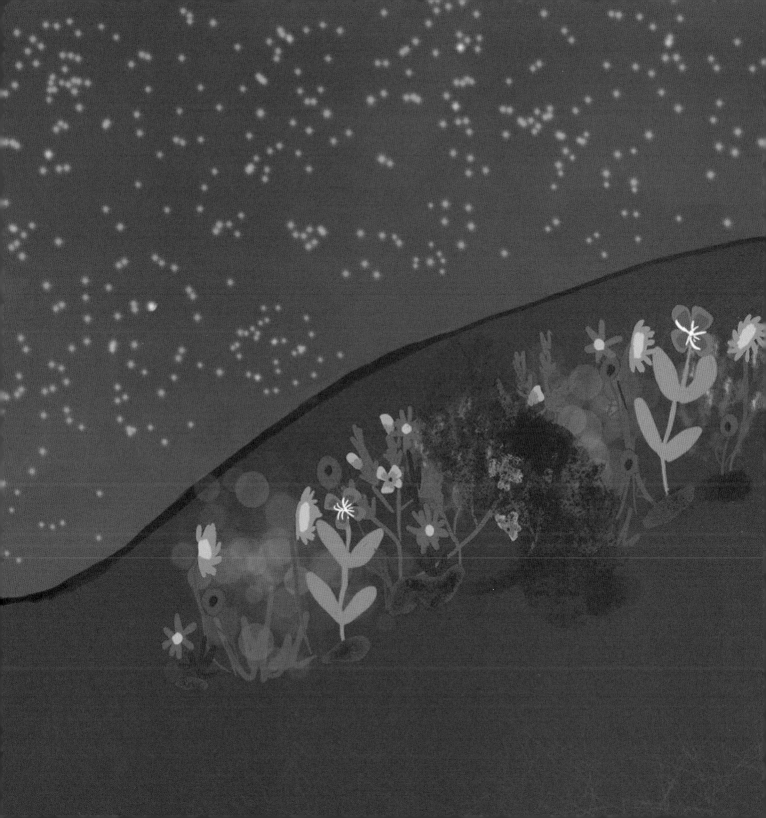

For Jameson and Bea
May all your dreams come true.
With love Mummy xxx

The Dream Room

With Little Lettie

April Moon

This is little Lettie. She should eat lettuces, but she likes chocolate the best.

Lettie lives underground with her Mummy, Daddy and the rest.

Lettie has a room which is cosy and round.

Where she sleeps on a night, nice and sound.

In her room there is a lamp and a bed.

In her house there is a livingroom and kitchen where everyone gets fed.

One morning Lettie awoke, and had a nice dream. She went to tell Aunt and Uncle while they ate their carrots and cream.

"My room should look like this, with a pink dinosaur, a carousel, a swimming pool, chocolates, flowers and more!"

Mummy and Daddy agreed they would try make her dream room come true. They would try make her burrow bigger, for big bunnies to get through.

It was time for a clear out. Mummy and Daddy said they would have to get rid of a large amount.

Lettie put away her toy train,
some bunnies and dummies,
books, and a photo frame.

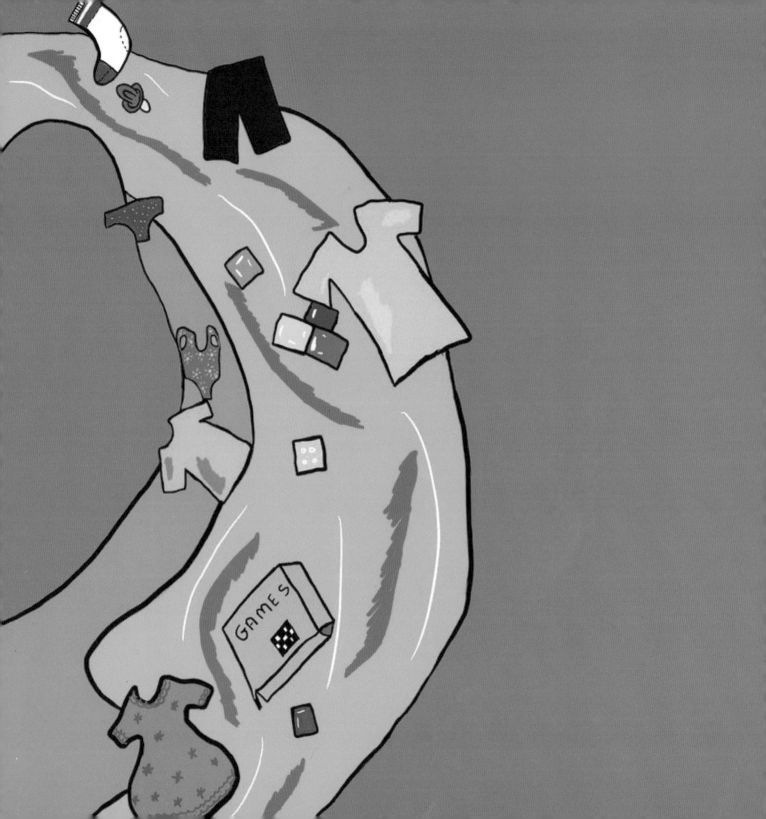

Grandma said: "In with the new, out with the old."
She gave her bed a lick of paint and her blankets a fold.

Wallpaper on.

"Lettie, close your eyes until all of it is done."

A lick of paint there....
The walls are no longer bare.

The special little light is bright.
"Put it on the bookshelf, Mum."
Aunty said.
Her dream room is nearly done.

Teddies on the bed.
Photos on the wall.
Doorways made tall.

Lettie, cover your
eyes...

"We have a big suprise!"
"Walk forward..."

All painted.
A tiny little dinosaur,
a lamp carousel,
some carrots, lettuces,
flowers and more.
"It was not quite what I had
in mind."
"But the little things I do
adore!"

Especially the floor!

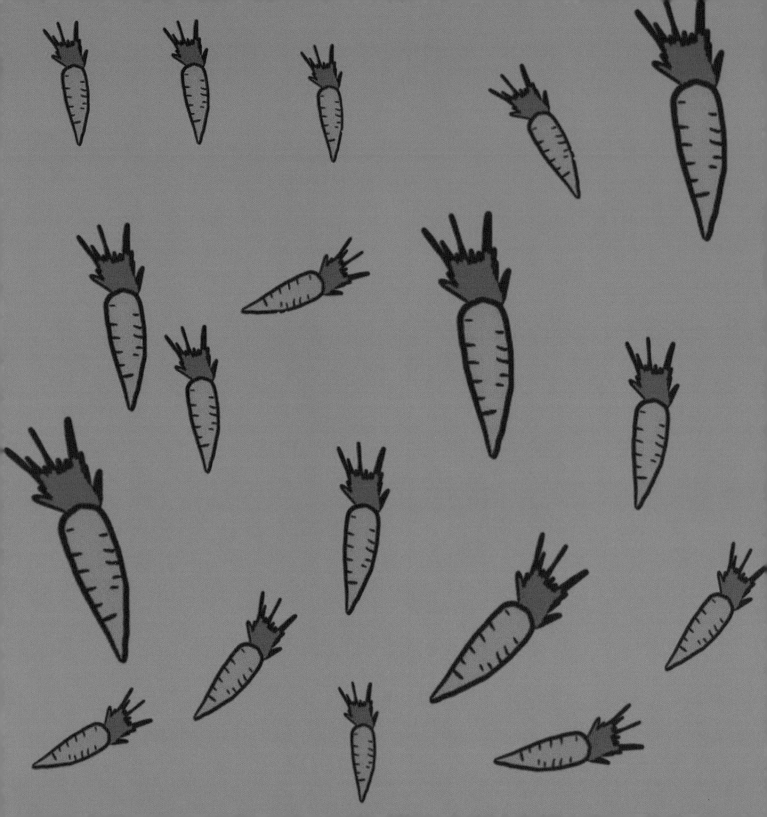

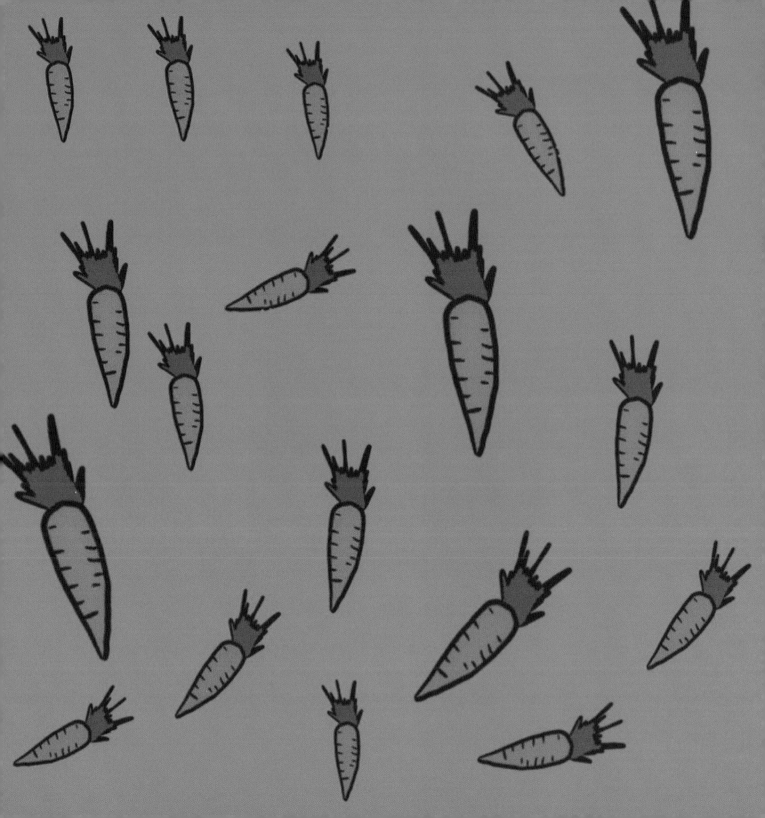

If you enjoyed this book follow along on with Lettie's adventures…

Instagram LettieLetsLearn

Draw pictures of Lettie for a chance to be shown.
Artwork from one of Lettie's biggest fans so far…

Thank you
To Bea
my daughter
for all
your love
and support.

Printed in Great Britain
by Amazon